Winnie-the-Pooh
Tiggers Don't Climb Trees

Adapted from the stories by A. A. Milne

One day, when Pooh was sitting on a stone in the middle of the stream thinking, he thought he would go and see Eeyore. He walked along, singing a little song to himself, then he thought he would go and see Owl instead as he hadn't seen him since the day before yesterday. But then he remembered Kanga, Roo and Tigger. And of course, there was Rabbit.

"I like talking to Rabbit," thought Pooh, and before he knew it, Pooh was back at his own front door again. It was eleven o'clock, which was Time-for-a-little-something . . .

Half an hour later, he was doing what he had always really meant to do, he was stumping off to Piglet's house.

Piglet was busy digging a small hole in the ground outside his house.

"Hallo, Piglet," said Pooh. "What are you doing?"

"I'm planting a haycorn, Pooh, so that it can grow up into an oak tree, and I'll have lots of haycorns just outside my front door, instead of having to walk miles and miles. Do you see, Pooh?"

"Supposing it doesn't grow up into an oak tree with lots of haycorns?" said Pooh.

"It will, because Christopher Robin says it will, so that's why I'm planting it."

Piglet put the acorn in the hole he had made, covered it with earth and jumped up and down on it.

When Piglet had finished jumping, he wiped his paws on his front and said, "What shall we do now?"

Pooh said, "Let's go and see Kanga and Roo and Tigger." So they set off for Kanga's house.

Kanga had felt rather motherly that morning and wanted to count things like Roo's vests, and how many pieces of soap there were left. So she sent Roo and Tigger out with a packet of watercress sandwiches for Roo and a packet of extract-of-malt sandwiches for Tigger. They were to have a nice long morning in the forest, not getting into mischief, and off they had gone.

As they went, Tigger told Roo all about the things that Tiggers could do.

"Can they fly?" asked Roo.

"Yes," said Tigger, "they're very good flyers, Tiggers are. Strornry good flyers."

"Ooh!" said Roo. "Can they fly as well as Owl?"

"Yes," said Tigger. "Only they don't want to."

Roo couldn't understand this, because he thought it would be lovely to be able to fly, but Tigger said it was difficult to explain to anybody who wasn't a Tigger himself.

"Can they jump as far as Kangas?" asked Roo.

"Yes," said Tigger. "When they want to."

In a little while, they came to the Six Pine Trees.

"I can swim," said Roo. "Can Tiggers swim?"

"Of course they can, Tiggers can do everything."

"Can they climb trees better than Pooh?" asked Roo, as they stopped under the tallest pine tree in the forest and looked up at it.

"Climbing trees is what Tiggers do best," said Tigger. "Much better than Poohs can."

"Could they climb this one?" asked Roo.

"I'll show you," said Tigger bravely, "you can sit on my back and watch me."

"Ooh, Tigger!" squeaked Roo excitedly. Then he sat on Tigger's back and they went up the tree trunk.

For the first ten feet, Tigger said happily to himself, "Up we go!"

For the next ten feet, he said, "I always *said* Tiggers could climb trees."

And for the next ten feet he said, "Not that it's easy, mind you."

And for the next ten feet he said, "Of course, there's the coming down too. Backwards!"

And then he said, "Which will be difficult . . . unless one fell . . . when it would be . . . EASY."

And at the word "easy", the branch Tigger was standing on broke, and he just managed to clutch onto the branch above him as he felt himself going . . .

Slowly, he scrambled upwards, until at last he was sitting on it, breathing quickly, wishing he had gone in for swimming instead.

Roo climbed off Tigger's back and sat next to him.

"Tigger," he said, excitedly. "Are we at the top?"

"No," said Tigger.

"Are we going to the top?"

"*No*," said Tigger, nervously.

"Oh!" said Roo, rather sadly. Then he went on hopefully, "That was a lovely bit when you pretended we were going to fall-bump-to-the-bottom, and we didn't. Will you do that bit again?"

"NO!" said Tigger, loudly.

Roo was silent for a little while. Then he said, "Shall we eat our sandwiches now, Tigger?"

Tigger said, "Yes, where are they?"

"At the bottom of the tree," said Roo.

"I don't think we'd better eat them just yet," said Tigger, so they didn't.

By-and-by, Pooh and Piglet came walking along.

"Look, Pooh!" said Piglet suddenly. "There's something in one of the pine trees."

"So there is!" said Pooh, looking up wonderingly. "There's an Animal."

Piglet took Pooh's arm, in case Pooh was frightened.

"Is it one of the Fiercer Animals?" Piglet said, looking the other way.

Pooh nodded. "It's a Jagular," he said.

"What do Jagulars do?" asked Piglet, hoping that they wouldn't.

"They hide in the branches of trees and drop on you as you go underneath," said Pooh. "Christopher Robin told me," he added.

Suddenly, the Jagular called out to them. "Help! Help!" it called.

"That's what Jagulars always do," said Pooh knowledgeably.

Something very excited next to the Jagular heard Pooh and squeaked, "Pooh and Piglet! Pooh and Piglet!"

"Pooh!" Piglet cried. "I believe it's Tigger and Roo!"

"So it is," said Pooh. "I thought it was a Jagular and another Jagular."

"What are you doing up there?" called Piglet.

"We can't get down, we can't get down!" cried Roo.

"How did you get there, Roo?" asked Piglet.

"On Tigger's back! And Tiggers can't climb downwards, because their tails get in the way. Tigger forgot about that when we started and he's only just remembered, so we've got to stay here for ever and ever – unless we go higher. What did you say, Tigger? Oh! Tigger says if we go higher, we shan't be able to see Piglet's house so well, so we're going to stop here."

"Piglet," said Pooh solemnly, "I think they're stuck." And he began to eat Tigger's sandwiches.

"Couldn't you climb up to them?" Piglet asked Pooh.

"I might, Piglet, and I might bring Roo down on my back, but I couldn't bring Tigger down. We must think of something else."

In a thoughtful way, Pooh began to eat Roo's sandwiches, as well.

Whether he would have thought of anything before he had finished the last sandwich I don't know, but he had just got to the last but one when Christopher Robin and Eeyore came strolling along together.

"There's Pooh!" said Christopher Robin. "Hallo, Pooh!" he said.

"It's Christopher Robin!" said Piglet. "*He'll* know what to do."

They hurried up to him.

"Oh, Christopher Robin," began Pooh.

"And Eeyore," said Eeyore.

"Tigger and Roo are up one of the Six Pine Trees, and they can't get down and –"

"And I was just saying," put in Piglet, "that if only Christopher Robin –"

"*And* Eeyore," said Eeyore.

"If only you were here, then we could think of something to do," said Piglet.

Christopher Robin looked up at Tigger and Roo and tried to think of something.

"*I* thought," said Piglet earnestly, "that if Eeyore stood at the bottom of the tree and Pooh stood on Eeyore's back, and I stood on Pooh's shoulders –"

"And if Eeyore's back snapped suddenly, then we could all laugh," said Eeyore, gloomily.

"Would it break your back, Eeyore?" asked Pooh, in surprise.

"That's what would be so interesting, not being quite sure till afterwards," said Eeyore.

Pooh said "Oh!" and they all began to think again.

"I've got an idea!" cried Christopher Robin suddenly. "I'll take off my tunic and we'll each hold a corner. Then Roo and Tigger can jump into it. They won't hurt themselves."

When Roo understood what he had to do, he was wildly excited. He cried out, "Tigger, we're going to jump! Tigger! Like flying, my jumping will be. Can Tiggers do it?" And he squeaked out, "I'm coming, Christopher Robin!" and he jumped straight into the middle of the tunic.

He bounced and bounced, and went on bouncing and saying "Ooh!" for quite a long time.

"Come on, Tigger," he called out. "It's *easy*."

But Tigger was holding tightly onto the branch.

"Just wait a moment," he said nervously, "there's a small piece of bark in my eye," and he moved slowly along the branch.

And suddenly, Tigger found how easy it was.

"Ow," he shouted as the tree flew past him.

"Look out!" cried Christopher Robin to the others.

There was a crash and a tearing noise, and then a confused heap of everybody on the ground.

Underneath everybody else was Eeyore.

"Oh, Eeyore!" cried Christopher Robin. "Are you hurt at all?"

Eeyore said nothing for a long time. Then he said, "Is Tigger there?"

Tigger was there, and he was feeling all bouncy again already.

"Yes," said Christopher Robin. "Tigger's here."

"Well, just thank him for me," said Eeyore.

This edition published in Great Britain 2002
First published in 2000 by Egmont Books Limited
239 Kensington High Street, London W8 6SA
Copyright © 2002 Michael John Brown, Peter Janson-Smith,
Roger Hugh Vaughan Charles Morgan and Timothy Michael
Robinson, Trustees of the Pooh Properties.
Published under licence from The Walt Disney Company.
Adapted from *The House at Pooh Corner*, first published 1928.
Text by A.A. Milne and line drawings by E.H. Shepard
copyright under the Berne Convention.
New and adapted line drawings and colouring of the illustrations
by Stuart Trotter copyright © 2000 Egmont Books Limited
All Rights Reserved.
ISBN 1 4052 0155 X
1 3 5 7 9 10 8 6 4 2
Printed in China.

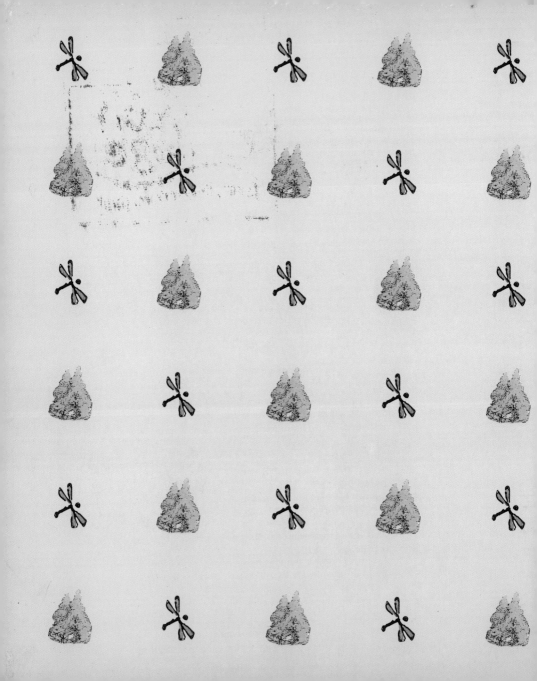